THE FLYING SHOES

THE FLYING SHOES

By Cynthia Jameson

Pictures by Lawrence Di Fiori

Parents' Magazine Press/New York

Library of Congress Cataloging in Publication Data

Jameson, Cynthia.
    The flying shoes.
    SUMMARY: Each successive person who tries to claim
the magic shoes stolen from the old man eventually wishes
he had never seen them.
    [1. Folklore—Russia] I. Di Fiori, Lawrence, illus.
II. Title.
PZ8.1.J3Fl   398.2'1'094787 [E]   72-8126
ISBN 0-8193-0642-8 ISBN 0-8193-0643-6 (lib. bdg.)

Especially for Louis

The tale of The Flying Shoes *comes from the rich folklore of the Udmurts, a Finno-Ugrian people who inhabit the western foothills of the Ural Mountains. Here the land is brilliantly green and much of the area is covered by thick forests. Here the winters are long and severely cold, the summers short and hot. As they have for many centuries, the Udmurts rely chiefly on goat and sheep raising for their livelihood. They have lived under Russian domination since the reign of Ivan the Terrible, but despite Russian efforts to convert them to Orthodoxy, they clung to their animistic faith, believing that spirits dwelt in all creatures, objects and natural phenomena such as thunder storms and earthquakes.*

The Udmurts are known for their distinctive styles in music and art as well as literature, and for many years their stories were passed on to young people by old storytellers, often accompanied by the lilting melodies of traditional folksongs. In the twentieth century they developed a written language and now many of these tales are available to students of folklore.

Long, long ago in the hills beyond a small village, there lived an old man who walked as swiftly as the wind.

Every year with the first blossoms of spring, he would come down from the hills to the village below.

On his humped back he carried great sacks filled with delicate herbs and sweet, wild roots. These he would bring to market to trade for a few eggs and cornmeal.

He never said a word, but would come and go, silently and mysteriously, like a cloud passing over the sun.

One fine summer day after the old man had traded all his roots and herbs at market, he set out on the long journey back to the hills.

Stopping to rest in a grove of birch trees, he sat on the moss and listened to the sounds of the forest.

Presently a young stranger came hobbling down the road in his direction.

"Old father," he hailed. "Let me sit by you and rest my poor, aching feet. I must carry this wood to my master and the road is long."

"My son," said the old man, "I do not wonder that your feet ache. For your shoes are nothing but holes!"

The youth looked at the old man's fine shoes and his eyes pricked with envy.

As if understanding the boy's thoughts, the old man added quickly, "Oh, no. My shoes are not new. They are nearly as old as my feet."

At this, the other's eyes widened with surprise.

"I wove them myself when I was a lad," the old man went on. "And I have always treated them kindly. I call them my flying shoes for they carry me over the earth with the speed of wings."

"These are the very shoes I need!" thought the youth. "Let the old one weave himself another pair. I shall steal these, first chance I get."

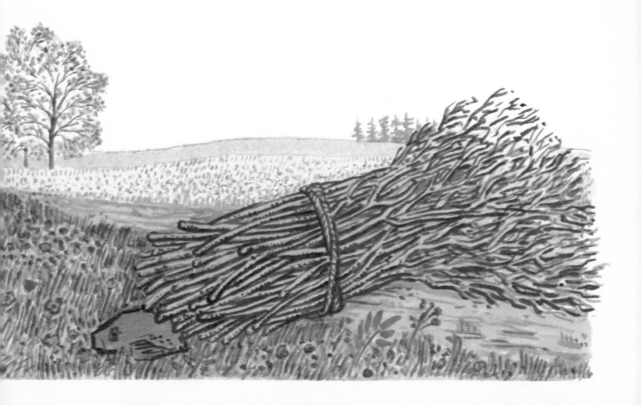

He did not have long to wait. The warm sun and the lazy droning of the bees soon lulled the old one to sleep.

Swiftly the youth removed the shoes and replaced them with his tattered ones. Then *he* put on the flying shoes.

But no sooner had he done this than he bolted up the road, quite unable to stop!

Suddenly houses and people appeared as a blur before his eyes. For he had swept through his village like a gust of wind.

With great effort, he turned himself about and headed back to the village and the house of his master.

Alas the shoes had a will of their own! The next instant, the youth found himself plunging headlong into a gully.

His legs thrashed wildly above his head, attracting droves of curious children.

"Help!" he cried in a frenzied voice. "My shoes—pull them off!"

Quickly the children flung themselves on his legs. They pulled and tugged till one shoe—then the other —popped off.

The youth stood up. Then tucking the flying shoes under his arm, he hurried barefoot to the house of his master.

When he arrived, he saw that the house was filled with guests.

The master, a rich merchant, scowled angrily at him. "Lazy fool!" he roared. "Where have you been with the firewood? You have kept our dinner waiting!"

He was about to flog the boy when suddenly his eyes lighted on the flying shoes.

"What magnificent shoes!" he thought. "I wonder how the young fool came by them? If only they were mine, how envious the others would be! I must find a way to get them..."

Suddenly an idea came to him—he would simply claim the shoes as his own!

And so in a loud voice he commanded, "Boy, bring my shoes here. I wish to wear them."

The youth froze with terror. "B-b-but, master..."

"Bring them here, I say!" stormed the merchant.

At this all heads turned to see what the shouting was about.

Meekly, the boy knelt and placed the flying shoes before his master.

How the guests marvelled! "They are stitched with threads of gold... How finely the leather is woven... They surely cost you a fortune..." chorused the voices.

Such admiration delighted the merchant. And he chuckled as he thrust his feet into the shoes. But, alas, no sooner done than up he sprang into a lively dance!

Madly he twirled about, leaping over tables and hopping up and down on the oven.

Thinking this was all in fun, the guests clapped their hands and stomped their feet.

And the more noise they made, the faster the merchant whirled round. "Stop me!" he wailed. "The shoes—they are cursed!"

After him rushed the guests, frantically clutching at the hem of his tunic.

And now the mad chase burst out the door and into the street.

Without warning, the merchant made a high leap and was caught on the branch of a tree.

There he hung, kicking helplessly, while the guests snatched at the flying shoes.

It so happened that at this very moment, down the village street came a fellow much disliked by everyone —the tax collector!

Dressed all in black, he moved very slowly, for his money bags weighed him down. Spying the goings-on, he shuffled toward the crowd to look closer.

"Eh? What's this?" he demanded of the unfortunate, upside-down merchant. "Are these scoundrels trying to steal your new shoes?"

"No, no," pleaded the merchant. "I do not want the shoes. *You* take them. Only, get them off me—quickly! O-o-o-oh..."

At this fine offer the tax collector threw himself on the merchant's legs and tugged at the shoes. Off came one—then the other.

Lest the merchant change his mind, the tax collector planted his own feet in the flying shoes. And the moment he did, up he rose straight into the air!

"Help! Help!" he shouted at the top of his voice. "Get me down!"

But the villagers just laughed and pointed their fingers at him.

In truth, they wished that he would never come down, for he taxed them till they were picked clean as bones.

And so the miserable fellow continued to float overhead, coattails flapping like great black wings.

All at once there fell upon the crowd a shower of gold coins!

Everyone saw how they were coming from the tax collector's money bags.

Forgetting where he was, the angry tax collector shook his fists and shouted threats at the people.

But the villagers went on filling their hats with joyful cries of, "More! More!"

In due time the tax collector drifted over to where the very poor villagers dwelt.

Here, upon the tumble-down huts, coins poured down in torrents.

Once the money bags were empty, the tax collector soared off in the direction of his own house.

When he arrived, he landed on the ground with a *thud*.

Even now the flying shoes gave him no peace. Round and round they made him run, about his house and field and cow.

"Catch me!" he cried breathlessly. And this his wife did—after some time.

Now, trembling with rage, the tax collector tore off the flying shoes. "These shoes are cursed!" he shrieked. "They caused me to lose all my money. I am going to send them back to the devil!"

And at once he climbed upon his roof and flung the shoes far into the air.

At first the flying shoes took a strange, zig-zag course and then circled above a birch grove.

Suddenly they dove, straight as arrows, down through the sunlight into the shadows of the tall trees.

Below, under one birch tree, slept an old man whose shoes were nothing but holes.

With a *thip* and a *thop*, the flying shoes fell to the ground and woke the old one with a start.

Slowly he picked up one—then the other—rubbing each fondly with his hand.

Then with a knowing smile on his lips, he slipped off the tattered shoes and put on his own flying shoes.

And now, once more he set off, as smoothly and gracefully as a bird taking flight, on the long journey back to his home in the hills.